The Father's Cabin

The Father's Cabin

Cheryl Olson

ISBN-13: 978-0-9988435-1-3

Published by Cheryl Olson Enterprises LLC
1867 Williams Hwy Ste 271
Grants Pass OR 97527

This book was edited by Lisa Thompson. You can email her at
writebylisa@gmail.com or visit her website at
www.writebylisa.com.

Cover designed by akira007 at fiverr.com.
Photograph of Bride by Nicole Ratliff Photography
Photograph of Bride is Kelsie Buckhorn
Illustrations in the book by Crystal Batten. Crystal's email is
crystalbatten77@gmail.com

All Scripture is taken from The Message (MSG)
Copyright © 1993, 1994, 1995, 1996, 2000, 2001, 2002 by Eugene
H. Peterson.

Ebook: Formatted by Steven Bremner
Paperback: Formatted by Alice Briggs

PART 1 - THE CABIN

CHAPTER 1

"Come with us tonight, Beth. You need the rest. You have nowhere else to go."

Beth looked around her, taking in the wreckage. Her small cottage stood in shambles, burned to the ground. She had managed to salvage her laptop and a few other items that were in her car, parked in the street. All the rest of her earthly possessions were lost in the fire.

Her father, Dave, had built the house with his own

hands from the ground up when he was a young man, spending hours to decide the placement of each nail and board as well as the positioning of the cupboards to make them accessible. He told story after story about his labor of love. When her parents passed away within months of each other, they left her this house--their legacy. As their only daughter, Beth had cherished this cozy home that now existed only in her memories. She now watched the smoke billowing out from flames that had been extinguished only moments before.

Beth shook her head, focusing again on the present. She glanced looking at the two men, her coworkers, as they patiently stood beside her, still waiting for her response.

The questions tumbled out. "How far is this place? How will I get to work each day?" While she could hardly stand the thought of returning to her job tomorrow, she didn't have the luxury of staying home.

"It's in the mountains, and of course, Beth, we'll take you to work if that's really what you want to do. I know the owner's son will be glad to bring you in if we can't make the trip. Will you come with us?" Merle and Gabe reassured her of their help.

Beth studied her two friends. Just weeks ago, the pair arrived at Awaken Insurance from the head office and now seemed to linger around her floor. Even now, she questioned how the two had arrived so quickly as she had been only standing here for moments, staring at the charred mess after emergency personnel had left. To them, it was just a routine call to another fire; to her, it was her world.

"Alright. I think I'd like to be with my friends now anyway. We can take my car." She fumbled in her bathrobe pocket, looking in vain for her keys. Too late, she remembered they were in their usual spot, hanging on the hook in the kitchen. They now lie buried in a burning pile of wood, fiberglass, wires and glass. She burst into tears once again. "My keys...they were in the house!"

Wrapping his strong arms around Beth, Merle held her while she sobbed. He smelled like jasmine and honeysuckle. "It's okay, Beth. We'll walk."

"Seriously?" Beth looked around the neighborhood, breaking from Merle's embrace. "You can't even see the mountains from here! It's a good 20 miles to the nearest campground, and we have to be at work in the morning. By the time we get there, we'll just have to turn around."

"Trust us, Beth." Both men gently took the laptop and miscellaneous possessions from her shaking hands. They stood calmly beside her, their comforting presence filling her with peace in the midst of the chaos. "Close your eyes."

She looked at them both in disbelief, then closed her eyes. When she opened them, they were standing in front of a forest. Shocked, she closed them again. The smell of the fresh pine needles, along with a combination of lavender and other scents, assaulted her senses. An owl hooted in the distance, confirming her presence in the woods. Feeling the dirt on her bare feet, she remembered that she hadn't put her slippers on when she left the house. She shivered in the chilly air. Blinking her eyes, she murmured, "How did we...."

"Hold our hands as we go through this part. The cabin is on the other side. Walking through Doubters' Hollow can prove challenging for first timers. And it's not the trail that's difficult."

Her two companions grabbed her hands tightly as she walked in step between them. Despite the dark and narrow path, the pair seemed to know their way, even without a flashlight. Her feet hit a few loose rocks along the path. Beth heard sounds but couldn't identify their source. Although she felt lost, peace tried to break though the fear that threatened to overwhelm her. She wanted to turn back, but her friends just held her tighter, and the peace that was fighting to break through now began to infuse her entire being. As they picked their way over the long trail, Beth wondered why they couldn't just close their eyes to reach the other side as they did before.

Doubters' Hollow seemed well named as a feeling of impending doom hung overhead. The noises behind them sounded like a rushing wind and grew louder as they continued their journey. As they walked farther, the forest darkened, enhancing her fears even more. Suddenly, at a clearing, the sound stopped.

"We have to go through the forest every time we come. It gets easier each time, and soon, you won't hear them."

"Them?" Beth asked.

"The Doubters."

"I don't want to go through that again," Beth tearfully replied. "I've never experienced anything like that. I don't even know how to describe what I felt."

"Someone will always be with you to keep you safe. If you ever go in by yourself, you will have to rely on your senses." Gabe responded reassuringly. Both he and Merle released her hands and gave back her laptop and bag. "The cabin is just up ahead. Most everyone has turned in for the night, but your room is ready."

"You mean you just assumed that I would come with you without checking with me first? That was certainly presumptuous!" Beth retorted. Her friends waited as she caught her breath. She stopped, glancing back at the dark forest as if she had second thoughts, hesitating before she looked ahead at the clearing. "I'll follow you." She announced quietly, reviewing her options.

A few minutes later, Beth's jaw dropped as they reached the cabin, which was unlike anything she had ever seen before. Set against an open field, the lights surrounding the perimeter twinkled with various colors, flowing like waves. The front porch wrapped around the entire first floor. Outside the front, the second floor also had a porch with French doors opening to the rooms above. Fresh scents lingered across the field, reminding her of safety and warmth and, well, *home*.

"Welcome, Beth!" A man in his early 30s stood up

from the front steps. Beth hadn't noticed him sitting there earlier. His long hair contrasted with the beard covering his face. His blue eyes shone as he gazed her with a look of recognition. Beth wasn't sure who he was although he seemed to know her. Even so, she didn't feel afraid as he approached her. "This is my Father's house, and we've been expecting you. Come in, and I'll show you to your suite."

"Suite? How did you know I would be here?" Beth queried again. She studied the man standing before her with renewed interest. He carried his tall frame with poise, wearing a pair of dark blue denim jeans and a green t-shirt.

"We just knew. By the way, my name is Joshua."

"Nice to meet you. But I'm a bit perplexed. I've never met any of you before. My friendship with Merle and Gabe has been mostly conversations around the water cooler. In fact, I'm not even sure how they knew where I lived." Beth turned around, but the pair had disappeared. "Where...."

"Let's get you settled." Joshua acted like Beth hadn't said anything. "You've had a trying night. You need food and rest."

Beth clutched her laptop and her bag but surrendered them to Joshua when he asked for them. He fell in step beside her as she walked to the porch.

Beth wasn't sure what to expect as she walked into the building. When Merle and Gabe first mentioned a "cabin," she imagined a rustic building that she hoped was had hot running water and no bugs. This went beyond her wildest expectations.

A few people circulated about, speaking in various languages. She felt as if she had been transported to the bar scene in "Star Wars" from years ago except these folks were more human than aliens.

"Hey there, Beth! How about a cup of tea?" Beth turned her head to the counter to the left of a bustling dining area. A middle-aged woman in a floral printed shirt nearly hidden by a white apron stood there smiling. Her hair, tinged with gray, was piled on her head.

"Would you bring her something to eat, Holly? I think she is pretty tired after her journey." Joshua asked for Beth. "Can you put together your famous chicken noodle soup for her? And some chamomile tea?"

"Certainly, Joshua. Actually, she looks like a chicken-and-stars kind of gal." Holly gave a wink, wiping her hands on her apron and continuing to the dining area just to her right to clean. Taking out a rag from the back pocket of her tan pants, she began wiping down tables.

Beth thought that Holly seemed energetic yet with a deeply sensitive soul. She gave off a lively yet comforting vibe. Beth continued to take in her surroundings, including a couple of people sitting in an alcove by a window with bowls lining the window sill. They appeared to be quietly chattering, but after a minute, Beth realized they were praying.

Joshua led her to a small room just down the hall

from the dining area with several racks of clothing. He picked out a few items and asked her to take them upstairs with her. While she knew this exchange should have been awkward anywhere else, it seemed perfectly natural here.

The elegant clothing felt soft in her hands as she carried them upstairs. Nothing like the starch polyester blue suit she wore to work every day. She made a mental note to ask Joshua about new work clothes since she had lost hers in the fire. Not that she was anxious about wearing them, especially when she held the silky garments in her arms.

Once at the top floor, Joshua stopped. "Here is your suite." He opened the French doors, and Beth gasped. The room, suitable for a princess, boasted shades of royal colors throughout. The sheer curtains on the windows were in deep hues of purples with gold trim, highlighting walls of light lavender with shimmering gold specks. The dressing table was covered with several bottles of lotions, perfumes, brushes and combs with large mirrors encasing the area. In a room off to the right, the bed stood invitingly with the balcony that she had seen earlier just to the other side of it. Next to the balcony door, a floor-to-ceiling wardrobe closet made of a rich mahogany with a gold inlay perfectly set off the elegant room. On the left, she heard water running in the bathroom. "I'll leave you in the capable hands of Celeste who will help you. I'll have Holly bring your soup and tea. Good night, Bethel."

Although she was stunned to hear her birth name, Beth didn't register her surprise. She responded, "Good night, Joshua, and thank you."

The relaxing bath made her drowsy, and she almost fell asleep in the warm water. She was used to taking quick showers, so the luxury of the tub seemed foreign. The water stayed warm, and the aromatic oils that Celeste had added helped calm her after the physical and emotional stress of the past few hours. Exiting the tub, she put on the over-sized robe hanging on the hook on the door and went into the outer room.

Celeste had laid out a long silk nightgown for her to wear, and she quickly changed. Beth was almost afraid to sleep in the bed for fear of ruining its luxury, but her tired body collapsed onto the smooth sheets of its own accord. Just as she pulled up the covers, she heard a knock at the door. Holly entered with a tray of soup and tea, setting it down on the dressing table. As she helped Beth settle in, she insisted, "I'll stay until you finish." She made herself comfortable, making conversation. "How do you like it here so far?"

"Lovely, a little overwhelming. Is Joshua always this forward?"

"He cares deeply about his guests. When someone visits, which isn't often, they seem to need what we have to offer."

"What it that?" Beth asked, sipping another bite of the savory broth. The soup, much like her mom made when she was a child, comforted her and filled

Cheryl Olson

her, beyond just the physical nourishment.

"Love. Unconditional, unadulterated love."

Joshua sat down on the top step of the porch, chatting with Merle and Gabe.

"Joshua, we tried to get to Beth's house before the fire started. The enemy beat us there." Merle reported.

"Don't worry; I know that you two did your best. I'll take care of it from here. At least Beth is safe now. Thank you for bringing her home."

CHAPTER 2

Rousing herself slowly, Beth realized she had overslept. At first, she thought maybe it was all a dream. The tea and soup had certainly hit the spot. When Holly had gathered up the tray, Beth nodded off, not even remembering that Holly had even left.

Opening her eyes, Beth noticed the sun shining brightly through her window. Despite the peacefulness of the cabin, she worried. She was always up before

13

dawn and out the door before the sun even peeped over the horizon. A nagging fear tugged at the corners of her mind--Doubters' Hollow. What or who lived there?

She jumped out of bed, racing to the wardrobe where Celeste had placed the pretty clothing Joshua had given her. Her basic blue polyester business suit hung there, cleaned and pressed. Beth groaned a little at the contrast of the outfits beside each other.

She wanted to stay at the cabin for the day instead of going to work. She turned the idea over in her mind but worried she was imposing on her hosts. Her company had firm rules in place that employees could not miss work unless they suffered a death in the family. She had seen some people drag themselves in with masks over their mouths, fighting off colds, flu, broken bones and similar misfortunes. Their branch worked hard to uphold their reputation of 100 percent participation.

Dressing hurriedly, she found her shoes in the closet, shining as if they were brand new. She slipped into a black trench coat that she found on a hook by the French doors. Thankful yet again that everything she needed was at her fingertips, she grabbed her laptop and cell phone off the nightstand and picked up a briefcase that looked just like the one lost in the fire.

Venturing out of the room and down the stairs, she ran into Holly wiping down the bar counter.

"I've got a bowl of oatmeal with your name on it, sweetie." Holly smiled as she turned toward the kitchen.

"Thanks, Holly, but I don't have time to eat. I need to

find Merle and Gabe so that they can walk me back to work. I just hope that we don't have to go back through Doubters' Hollow."

"Oh! Merle and Gabe are on a new assignment as of last night." Beth turned toward Joshua, entering the front door with his guitar. He set the instrument down on a bench by the door. Beth could see the couple sitting in the alcove. She wondered again what they were doing.

"They are answering prayers." Joshua responded to her thoughts. "I'll take you to work from now on."

"Thanks, but I don't want to impose. You've already been so generous! I'm sure I could stay at a motel until the insurance adjuster finishes."

"Nonsense, you are our guest. We want you here! We designed the suite upstairs especially for you." Holly responded as she brought out the bowl of oatmeal. "Now eat." She insisted.

Holly glanced over at Joshua. "When you go through the Doubters' Hollow, can you pick my herbs?"

"Certainly. Any other requests? Do you need flowers?"

"Yes, please. Pink lady slippers. And violets. I'm going to make essences out of them for our guest." Holly replied, pouring a cup of tea for Beth.

"I didn't know you could make essences from pink lady slippers." Beth took another bite of the oatmeal, savoring the unique blends of sweet fruits.

"We can make essences from any plant," Holly replied. "Every plant has its own healing purpose. The

15

Father knew that whatever he chose to create, the enemy came to steal, kill and destroy. He had an alternate plan."

"I really need to leave for work. We have to be there promptly at 8:00." Beth looked at Joshua again. She didn't see a clock, but she knew she would be late by the angle of the sun outside the cabin door.

"Let's go!" Joshua helped Beth off her stool. The pair murmured a quick goodbye to Holly and the others. The couple in the alcove ignored them as they continued praying, each holding a bowl in their laps.

Walking through the field towards Doubters' Hollow, Beth and Joshua chatted. Even so, she felt that he already knew everything about her. Just before entering the forest, Beth hesitated as Joshua kept walking. He glanced over his shoulder, calling out, "When I walk through, the voices are quiet. Enjoy the stroll at your leisure."

While she still felt the tension from the previous night, Beth began to relax as she watched him wander around, gathering flowers and herbs for Holly. The night before, Beth couldn't take in her surroundings, so she only knew this trail. In the light of day and without the voices to distract her, she was able to see the beauty of the forest. Looking around at the gorgeous canopy, she wondered why the voices had seemed so threatening just hours ago. Rose bushes and other flora spread out around her as though a professional gardener had cultivated them.

Joshua read her thoughts. "The doubters can't see the forest through the trees. They have no idea what is down here as they can only see from one perspective. They swing from one tree to the next. Once in a while, someone will fall out, and the others climb down and pull them back up."

"That is so sad. Look at how the beauty from the field blends in. Holly created this entire area herself. She often comes here as well. No wonder she picks flowers and herbs from here."

As she continued walking, wider trails intersected with the one she was on. "Where do these other trails lead?"

"People venture into the forest without knowing about the cabin or about Doubters' Hollow. If they haven't accepted my invitation to join us, they think other ways lead to the cabin. They don't want to follow the main path. As you see, some are just dead ends while others take travelers deeper into the forest. They listen to the voices instead of using our guides. Never come here without a guide, or you will find yourself on one of these trails, lost. If you do find yourself on your own, lean on your senses to find your way. The journey will be treacherous, but you will make it to the other side in one piece. Learn the main trail that takes you where you need to go."

At the end of the forest, Joshua asked Beth to close her eyes. "For those who come at my invitation, I show you a different way than those who 'find the forest' on their own."

When she opened her eyes, she stood at the front door of her work building. Joshua walked with her inside the lobby. Beth introduced him to the main-floor manager, Raul, as they stood visiting with Maggie, the front desk manager.

"We've met before," Joshua replied, shaking Raul's hand.

"We have?" Raul asked.

"Yes. I oversee all my Father's businesses. You helped arrange for my Father's artifacts to be brought here and put on display in the lobby." Joshua pointed to a table made of gopher wood and seven lamps scattered around the seating area in the lobby. Other items were strategically placed there as well. Beth noticed tears forming in Joshua's eyes. The questions sprung to her lips, but she would ask them later.

"Oh, those. Of course." Raul replied, clearing his throat. "That was an event for sure."

Joshua looked around the lobby. "I noticed that some of my Father's treasures are not in the proper location."

He waited for Raul to offer an explanation to no avail. Apparently, he didn't seem to realize the importance of where each item was positioned.

After another questioning glance at Raul, Joshua stated, "I'll be back to pick you up later, Beth." Joshua bid goodbye to the group.

After Joshua left, and Beth entered the "inner sanctum," Maggie and Raul left the building together, unseen. The early morning hour provided a cover for their clandestine rendezvous as the others settled in at work. No one left the room until the day was over at 5:00 p.m. as per the new rules, instituted by headquarters a few months ago. Raul had suggested to Maggie that this was the perfect time to find some privacy since upper management never left the building until lunch. That gave them plenty of time before Maggie's husband, the church pastor, came to pick her up for lunch.

Raul impressed Maggie the first time she met him. As the pastor's wife at Resurrection church for the last three years, he just showed up as they were moving into the parsonage. Raul's easy-going personality drew Maggie to him. However, pastor didn't feel so sure. Despite his cautions, Maggie ignored her husband's requests concerning Raul as the two of them worked together at Awaken Insurance.

When they arrived at the hotel as per their usual routine for the past six months, Raul found a table in the lobby where they sat for breakfast before they went up to their room.

***

Beth looked at the clock in the lobby and realized that, despite her concerns, she wasn't late to work. The cabin seemed to affect the passage of time. It was a new day, yet her heart still broke over losing her childhood home. She didn't know where she would go tonight when she was done with work.

She went to her own cubicle in the inner sanctum where she found a lovely bouquet of flowers from the company. She glanced at the card, which read, "We are sorry for the loss of your home. We have made arrangements for you to stay in one of our vacation properties on the beach until your home is rebuilt."

She opened the envelope with the map and a key to the beach house. Thankful for their kindness, she smiled at the company's care of her, remembering their similar generous treatment when her parents were sick. Due to their terminal diagnosis and the fact that they were both top managers in the company, Beth was granted an exception to take time off with pay to care for them.

As comforting as the gesture was, Beth felt that something was amiss as she thought about it. She admittedly craved solitude and enjoyed living alone. Even so, she loved the pampering she had received from Celeste and Holly at the cabin. She realized that the company had not tried to reach out to her during the night. Her cell was with her the entire time, and even though the cabin had no reception, she had no missed calls or emails when she checked her phone that morning. The discrepancy in the actions of upper management nagged at her throughout the day. Finally, she brought up the matter with Sara, who worked in the next cubicle.

"I heard about the fire, Beth. I went by the property,

but you must have already left. I'm surprised you came in today."

"I stayed with some people from the office. They came by when it happened. I thought about calling you as I didn't want to impose on them. But they were very insistent and kind."

"I'm so glad they were there for you." Sara replied. Before Beth could say anything else, Sara's email alert dinged, and she turned around her chair.

Throughout the day, Beth looked for Merle and Gabe, but she didn't see them. Normally, she ran into them at the water cooler or on break. She finally decided they weren't in, but the irony of their absence didn't escape her.

At first, Maggie hadn't realized that Merle and Gabe were from corporate headquarters. She refused to let them into the inner sanctum, the area reserved for the most elite employees. Employees--and everyone else-- had to strictly adhere to a specific dress code to even walk past the gates. Men and women alike needed to don a blue suit with a white shirt and black shoes. Women wore their hair in a stylish cut but could not have braids. The men had to be clean shaven. With their khakis, polo shirts, Birkenstocks and beards, Merle and Gabe missed the dress code by a mile. After more than an hour of convincing and several phone calls, they were finally admitted. Their regular appearance at meetings with floor managers as they roamed the facility had made for some interesting topics over the last several weeks.

During her lunch hour, Beth managed to make some calls to the insurance company concerning the house and its belongings. She faxed them the report from the fire department and then went to the break room. After grabbing a sandwich from the vending machine, she sat down, and Sara walked in.

"So where did Merle and Gabe take you?" Sara asked as she warmed her soup.

"They took me to a beautiful and spacious cabin. But it didn't have cell reception or internet."

"Where is it?"

"To tell you the truth, Sara, I really don't know. We just started talking and walking, and the next thing I knew, we had arrived. They introduced me to Joshua, the overseer. He's associated with the company, but I'm not exactly sure how. Anyway, he's coming by to pick me up after work. The beach house sounds beautiful, but I really love staying at the cabin. I think it's healthy for me to be around Joshua, Holly and the others. Do you want to join us and see it for yourself?" For a moment, Beth forgot about Doubters' Hollow. Once she thought about it again, she realized how safe she felt as she walked through it with Joshua.

"Maybe another time. It sounds too 'granola' for me." Sara laughed. "Besides, I've seen Merle and Gabe. Are they the type of people you want to hang out with?" Sara asked. "I know they are apparently part of the company, but they aren't really the type of people we associate with. I'd be leery of them even if they are friends with the boss' son. They don't fit in with the rest of us. I mean, those clothes! And their beards! What will people think if they see you together?"

Sara's words went in one ear and out the other. Beth couldn't explain the peace that she had felt at the cabin--unlike anything she'd experienced before. She could finally relax and "let her hair down." Trying to explain those feelings to Sara would be an effort in futility.

At the end of the day, Joshua was waiting for her in the lobby. "Ready?" He asked as he got up.

"Yes. If it's okay I'd like to go by my property once more. I know I'm imposing on your generosity but...."

"I totally understand." Joshua assured her. "I like to come to the city once in a while and see where I used to reside."

"You used to live here?"

"I've lived many places." Joshua opened the door for her as they walked down the busy street. He pointed to a church at the end of the block. "I helped build Resurrection Church with my own two hands and was welcomed there as I worshiped my Father. However, I did some things that made them uncomfortable, so they asked me to leave." Joshua stared at the tall building.

"What were they so afraid of?"

"Freedom." Joshua answered.

The church door was unlocked, and Joshua held it open for Beth as they entered. "In all of the homes my

Father and I built, the common denominator is the love for my Father. The congregants have issues among themselves, yet they ignore the builders. That's what separates us from some occupants." They sat down in a pew.

"I thought you were kicked out of this church." Beth wondered.

"The pastor is an old friend, so he lets me come in to sit and pray. However, some in the congregation don't want me here. They hold most of the decisions by their pocketbook.

"Others here have listened to my call going out to other parts of the world to tell of my Father's love, but meanwhile, some feel they can serve me better with a checkbook even though they try to limit the spending. I never told anyone to base their giving on if the missionaries go to foreign lands for two weeks or two years. Some who have been called haven't gone yet because of tight purse strings, but I'm working on a way to send them."

"How?"

"Close your eyes."

Suppressing a giggle, Beth obeyed.

"Open them." Beth could hear chattering voices and panicked, thinking she was in the forest again. But when she opened her eyes, she gasped and looked to her right where Joshua had been sitting only moments ago. He was gone. "Where...." She realized that the people around her didn't seem shocked at her sudden appearance. She sat on a bench inside a mall she didn't recognize.

At first, Beth wondered she was near the town she lived in. She listened closely before determining that the language she was hearing actually Mandarin. The bright lights of the stores glared as shoppers rushed about the courtyard area. She felt a peace there and didn't want to close her eyes again as this fascinated her.

Beth considered getting up and walking over to the food court as the pork rice and Mar Far chicken smells drew her but decided against it. She didn't know if this was a portal and had never experienced this before except when they had traveled to the cabin the previous night.

"I'm ready to come back, Joshua." She whispered so that no nearby bystanders would hear her.

She instinctively closed her eyes again. When she opened them, she was sitting back in the pew in the church with Joshua next to her.

"What happened?" she asked.

"Holly and I do that together. It's called traveling in the spirit. You've been going to the forest and to the city using this method over the last couple of days."

"And anyone can do it?"

"If they believe, yes."

Beth pondered Joshua's words as they left the church and continued down the street. After some minor chit chat about the area, Beth asked him a question that had plagued her all day. "How do you know Raul? I sensed some tension between the two of you this morning."

"Beth, once you get to know me, you will find I have no issue with anyone. I love everyone unconditionally. Raul has an issue with me and my Father. It's a power struggle, and he won't win." Joshua took a deep breath. "You've seen the articles in the lobby? As you know, the man that my Father picked for CEO of the company was your father. He was in charge of bringing my Father and his things to the company building when it was finished. Dave had planned out everything for a long time. However, my Father moves according to certain procedures. Dave didn't pay attention to what my Father wanted and did his own thing.

"Dave planned the celebration, but everything was out of order. Raul and his brother had put my Father in the back seat of an expensive convertible. They drove over a rock in the road, and Raul's brother reached out to steady Father. In the process, Raul's brother fell out of the car, landing on his head and dying.

"My Father grieved over the death and stopped the celebration to stay with some family friends. Dave and my Father handled everything for Raul and his family and then proceeded to start again with the celebration.

"My Father needs a place where he can interact with his people. It saddens him when people don't include us in their plans.

"After three months of staying with friends, Dave decided to follow my Father's plan to the letter. On that wonderful day, we had a parade through town, and my

Father was able to meet with those that followed him."

Beth interjected. "About Raul's brother. Does Raul hold you and your Father responsible?"

"If he does, he shouldn't. He didn't follow directions to the letter. If he had, the accident wouldn't have happened." Joshua responded.

"So your Father owns the beach house as well." Beth observed. "Why couldn't I stay there?"

"Yes, my Father owns that home and many others. The problem is that I'm not always invited to the homes he owns and at times, neither is he. Remember the trails that I showed you in Doubters' Hollow? It's very similar here. People should use what my Father gave them, even the church, for his purpose and his pleasure, but instead, they use it for their own selfish reasons and defile all that he has done for them. Like the trails the Doubters have forged in the forest to lead them to the cabin, they will end in disaster instead without my Father's aid."

Beth pondered on his words and was still lost in her thoughts when they arrived at where her house once stood. Looking at what was now a bare lot, Beth asked, "Who cleaned it all up?" She struggled to speak through her tears. "I called the insurance company at lunch but didn't think they would work this fast."

"It's been taken care of, Beth," Joshua took her in his arms. She continued to sob for several minutes as the events of the last 24 hours finally sunk in. "We did find several things still intact from the fire and set them to the side over by the fence behind a bush." He led her to the area, showing her the items.

Although the pile was small, nothing smelled of smoke despite the proximity to the charred remains of her beloved home. The salvaged contents included a family picture of Beth with her parents taken shortly before her father had passed. She had no more photos as her mother had grown extremely weak after her father's death.

After their deaths, she had dated some. But the boys that she dated were just that--boys. She needed a man. She admitted to playing games here and there herself, but nothing seemed to fill the aching void. She longed for a life partner but pushed appropriate suitors away. At the same time, she kept dating the wrong guys as her loneliness grew. Even though she was scared of making a wrong choice, she did what she wanted, despite the consequences.

Forcing herself to come back to the present, she looked again at the pile of belongings. She found a necklace that she had worn most of her adult life along with the metal safe that held all the insurance papers and investment information. Beth was surprised that none of the items had been looted. And then she noticed them--Merle and Gabe stood guard next to the pile.

"Insurance paid all the medical bills. As far as the house, they will only pay me for its value and not for any of the contents. I'm still not sure if I will rebuild." Beth mumbled to herself.

"Did you clean all of this up?" Beth asked. "Was this your new assignment?"

Gabe, who was leaning against the fence, sat up and laughed. Their blue t-shirts and dark jeans with red suspenders complemented their blonde hair, which was covered by wide brim hats to protect them from the blazing sun.

Both men rose as Merle glanced at Joshua. "We're going back to the cabin."

Beth turned from the pile she was sorting through to say goodbye, but true to form, they had vanished. She smiled to herself, thinking about her own experience only moments before. She was learning a new method of transportation, which took some adjusting.

Beth stood up, looking back at the pile as she walked away. "I just want this picture and my necklace. And the safe, of course. Maybe I could go to the beach house until the insurance pays me to rebuild."

"Do you want to?" Joshua asked. He joined her as she left the devastated scene.

"Honestly, no. I felt so safe last night as if all my fears had melted away. I have never experienced anything like that before." Beth replied. "And Holly's soup was amazing."

"Holly has been with me since the beginning. She actually roams in your world more than anyone. Instead of the bartender, we call her Holly the heart tender because of her work at the cabin, but what she does out here is even more amazing."

Almost without noticing it, they arrive at a park and found a worn bench where they could sit. As Joshua continued his story, Beth glimpsed something familiar about him that tugged at her memory but then brushed it off.

"Holly visits people during the darkest times of their lives and reaches into the depths of their souls to heal them from the pain life gives them."

"What about me? Did she visit me when my parents died?" Beth's voice cracked with emotion as she stared at her shoes, afraid of the answer.

"Yes, she did." Joshua replied. "She's been with you the whole time. She arranged for Merle and Gabe to help you last night."

"This is all so surreal." Beth sighed as she raised her eyes. "I love being at the cabin, but if Holly knew everything that I think about, she wouldn't want me there. Why have you chosen me?"

"Actually, you chose me as a young child years ago. Do you remember?"

***

Flashback--20 Years Ago

Six-year-old Beth sang along with her mother and father. As she looked up from the hymn book, she spotted a tall man dressed in a robe, standing behind the pastor. The man looked out over the congregation, and tears fell from his eyes. "Mama, why is that man crying?" She whispered. Her mother glanced up from the hymn book at the pastor and could see that the pastor was blocking the man, who was trying to make his presence known.

Tears formed in her mother's blue eyes. Beth looked around in wonder at the rest of the congregation. Everyone else had their noses buried in their hymnals. They weren't paying any attention to the man behind the pulpit. Beth's mom sensed her daughter's rising fear. She reassuringly put her hand on Beth's knee as she whispered to Beth, "This is a sad day for all of us." Beth looked up at her mother again, a question in her eyes. She liked how neatly her mom styled her blond hair, pulled back into a bun that rested at the nape of her neck. Beth placed her little hand on her mother's blue dress as she tried not to worry. The man that was trying to get the pastor's attention had fire in his eyes, but he seemed so kind and loving. She looked up again, and he seemed to stare straight into her heart, reading all her secrets. Warmth and peace washed over her, and she relaxed as she joined in the chorus again.

***

Present Day

"Oh my goodness!" Beth gasped. "That was you! I'm so sorry!" The realization hit Beth as she began to cry.

Cheryl Olson

"They didn't even see you! Why not?"

"Because they didn't know me. But you did."

Beth mulled over his words, not even noticing that they had gone through Doubters' Hollow.

They stopped at the door, and Beth bid Joshua good night, thanking him for bringing her back to the cabin.

As Beth climbed the stairs, Joshua loitered on the porch, gazing over the serene landscape as dusk settled. Merle made his way up the steps, standing beside Joshua. "She will realize who she is." Merle observed.

"Indeed. Yet my heart breaks for what she will suffer before she comes to that realization."

Just then, Holly stepped out the cabin's front door. "Thank you, Joshua, for the pink Lady Slippers. I'm on the hunt for violets and honeysuckle for our guest."

"Thank you, Holly, for taking such good care of her and for preparing her to be my Bride."

***

From the bedroom window, Beth stared at the bright light in the forest. She glanced up, catching a glimpse of sinister figures in the trees and wondered why she hadn't seen them that morning with Joshua. She watched as Holly picked flowers from the ground. Surrounded by the bright light that seemed to radiate from her, she ignored the swirling shadows above her.

Beth was beginning to feel at home here although she knew her stay would just be temporary. A sense of warmth and peace washed over her, one that she hadn't felt in years. She knew there was something familiar about it, but she concentrated on everything she had to do. She wanted to move back to her cozy house as soon as possible. She was grateful to Merle and Gabe for cleaning up the place and noticed that they hadn't used any equipment. She wanted to ask them how they had accomplished the task so quickly. The charred wreckage alone should have taken hours to move under normal circumstances. Even so, she was slowly beginning to realize that events surrounding the cabin and Joshua himself weren't "normal."

As Beth crawled into the cozy bed, she again wondered about Joshua and who he was. Everything seemed surreal, yet she was comfortable with the situation. She wished that she didn't have to move on, but she still didn't feel like she totally belonged at the cabin, either.

***

Flashback--20 Years Ago

Later that evening, Beth's father and mother sat down on the couch and explained that they would not be attending Resurrection Church for the time being. Beth looked at her father, a tall, slender man. His hair was starting to turn gray in some places, and her mother often joked that it was from slaying giants that were after the things that the Father himself cherished. Dave carried the heart of the Heavenly Father in his own. This move from the church would affect them all, but Beth didn't need to worry as they would always show her who Joshua was.

***

She knew now that they left Resurrection Church right when Joshua was kicked out.

She felt herself drift off to sleep and let herself float into relaxation.

Holly bent down to pick a few daisies when she felt a tickle on her back. Looking up, she saw a Doubter.

"Are you okay?" She asked.

"What do you care?" it snarled.

Holly looked at the figure before her, which appeared to be just a boy. "You seem too young to be here." Holly whispered.

"Maybe I am. Why do you keep messing around here?"

"The Father put in this garden for me."

"There is no Father! You're making that up."

"Oh, my child, yes, there is, and he loves you and everyone in here. His heart breaks because you don't want to know him."

"Don't listen to her, Zach! It's all lies!" A voice above them hollered. "Get back up here!"

Holly looked at the boy and could see that he was

softening. "Does someone really love me? Me?"

"Zach! Get up here now!" The orders grew even sterner as the voice yelled more loudly.

Holly gazed at Zach, compassion reflected in her eyes. Placing her hand on his shoulder, she announced, "Yes, my child, there is." Holly turned him around to face the cabin. "Would you like to walk with me to see his Son?"

"Zach! What are you doing? Come on! Guys, we need to get him back up here! Zach, don't listen to her! You can't go with her!"

Ignoring their cries, Zach left the forest, their voices fading in the distance. As he walked toward the cabin, Joshua waited on the porch. Zach began to sprint across the field, compelled by an unspeakable love that reached across the field to him from the cabin. As Zach ran into Joshua's arms, tears flooded his cheeks. The love emanating from Joshua overwhelmed him, and he never wanted to let go of this feeling.

CHAPTER 3

Two days later, Beth sat at her desk, puzzled. She held a check from the insurance agent although she hadn't expected it quite so soon. Staring, her eyes grew blurry. Lost in her thoughts, she jumped when someone behind her coughed.

Turning around, she looked up at her supervisor. "Raul! My apologies. I didn't hear you."

"Beth, how are you doing? Where are you staying?"

Cheryl Olson

"I'm staying with friends who have given me a room of my own at their cabin until my house can be rebuilt."

"I remember now; you are staying with Joshua," Raul commented. "Didn't the company offer you the beach house?" His mouth twitched a little. Raul didn't have much of a poker face, and Beth suspected that he knew more than he was letting on.

"Yes, they did, and I am grateful. Perhaps later, if it's still available." Beth looked up at the clock.

"I've got several files to go through before 5:00. Was there anything else?"

"I was curious. Have you seen any more pictures from our retreat last month? I'm making a bulletin board and wanted everyone's pictures for a collage."

"I didn't take any. But Sara uploaded several pictures onto the business website. You could check there to see what she has."

Raul hesitated, still staring at her, his expression unreadable. Still, something about his eyes made her uneasy.

"What?"

"Nothing. Again, if you need anything, don't hesitate to call."

"I will, Raul. Thank you."

Beth turned back to her desk, putting the check in the envelope and then into her purse. She then settled herself, focusing on the last few remaining files on her desk. Despite her good intentions, her mind wandered back to the cabin.

She had met Zach that morning before work. At 12, he seemed very active. Holly explained what had happened in Doubters' Hollow.

"Every once in a while, a doubter falls out of the trees. Some follow the other trails, trying to reach the cabin but end up back in the trees. Zach is the first one to come here." Holly replied. "He's a hungry boy. A baseball game is starting, and he plays short stop." Holly was enjoying doting on Zach, and Beth could see that Zach loved every minute of it.

"There's some tea, eggs and a biscuit for breakfast on the counter. Why don't you come join us?"

"I think I will." Beth agreed. She was genuinely curious about the exchange between Holly and Zach. She reflected further on the relationship between the doubters and Joshua. She had thought they were enemies, but watching Holly and Zach, she knew her assumptions were wrong.

As Beth looked around the dining area, she noticed a gate on the east side of the cabin for the first time. She asked Holly about it, listening while she ate.

"When the cabin was built, the Father put in the gates to represent the gate in the temple in Jerusalem. This gate, called the Mercy Gate, has never been opened and won't be until Joshua comes to get His Bride."

Beth studied the gates more closely. Even from afar, she noticed the detail on the wooden doors. As she looked through the gates, she smiled. They bore the same logo that the company used on nearly everything they released, from their stationary to the outside of the policy and procedure manuals. Her father had designed the logo. Her thoughts went back to Holly's statement.

"Joshua's engaged?" Beth asked. The surprise--and disappointment--showed in her eyes. She quickly dropped her gaze, hoping that Holly hadn't seen her true feelings.

"In a matter of speaking, yes." Holly answered.

"Beth, do you have the Martin file, by chance?" Sara peaked out from around the cubicle wall, startling Beth out of her reminiscing.

"Let me check." Beth opened up a file cabinet. "Here it is. I wanted to make sure that everything was in order." Beth rose from her chair, handing the file to Sara. "I invited Jill to the group picnic next month. I know that she quit drinking a couple of months ago, but her husband is in rehab, so he won't be able to make it," Beth commented. "Jill told me that she hopes they can come together the next time."

"As long as they have quit smoking. I hate picking up those butts in the park when we leave. Plus it gives us a bad reputation when people see us with our clients lighting up at the park." Sara closed the file. "How would you like to start off the weekend at "Shenanigans" tonight for a girls' night? We'll probably be out late. What do you think about joining us?"

Beth thought about her question for a moment. She could use the distraction of spending time with some friends. She hadn't done that in months. Even so, she hesitated, concerned about Joshua's feelings. What would he think if she came home so late? She regretfully declined. "Thanks for the kind offer. Maybe next time."

Right at 5:00, Joshua arrived to pick her up. Beth smiled as he opened the door for her, and she walked into the fresh air. As he chatted about the evening ahead, Beth was glad that she'd decided to stay in. She enjoyed his friendship and their relaxed conversations.

"Tonight's dinner will be off the charts. Holly cooks a great brisket with a side of potatoes and green beans, grown in our garden. Her tender heart is part of the reason that it tastes so delicious."

"Sounds lovely." Beth replied as they continued down the block. "And for dessert, angel food cake?"

Joshua laughed. "I think you are getting the idea."

Beth had a couple of hours before dinner, so she decided to take advantage of the remaining daylight to explore the cabin further. She walked past the counter and the kitchen area to a separate porch. As she opened the glass doors and stood outside at the back of the cabin, several small villages dotted the landscape in the distance, as far as she could see. To the left, a white gazebo invited her to take advantage of the warmth of the setting sun. Closing her eyes, she sat down on the bottom step. The sun slid behind the mountain range to the west. Holly noticed her there and joined her at the gazebo.

"Isn't this the perfect spot to enjoy the beauty?" Holly asked.

"Why didn't I notice this view before?" Beth queried.

"Sometimes we are so wrapped up in our earthly cares that we forget to look at what is right in front of us." Holly motioned to the right. "Beyond that hill is Doubters' Hollow. They can't even see all the beauty this place holds."

"Why are they there, and why does the Hollow exist?"

"That's where the Doubters go. They are right on the brink of believing but rely on their logic and what their eyes can see instead of trusting in the Father."

The pair sat for a minute in companionable silence, watching the sun slide into the mountains as the shadows spread across the field. Finally, the air grew chilly. Holly rose to her feet. "You'd best get ready for your dinner date." The pair returned to the warmth of the cabin.

Celeste had selected a blue silk gown for her to wear to dinner that evening. Beth wondered about the formality of the dress as the dining room was not that elegant. However, she shrugged off her questions and decided to go with the flow. Although she was never sure what to expect, she enjoyed the dreamlike atmosphere of life at the cabin. Celeste styled her long blond hair into a ponytail and proceeded to shape a bun into a rose at the nape of her neck. Again, Beth wondered at the elegant style that seemed excessive for the casual atmosphere of the cabin.

Once at the dining room, she noticed the change in

décor from informal to understated elegance. A crystal chandelier floated above a single table. Sitting there, Joshua cut a striking figure, wearing a dark gray suit. He rose when Beth entered, smiling his approval. She blushed despite admitting to herself how welcome his attention felt.

Her mind flashed back to past relationships. No one had ever treated her as kindly as Joshua had. In high school, her dad insisted that the boys she dated came to the door, but she ignored his request. She knew that he would not approve of the guys that she was seeing. Yet not one of them treated her as a woman of value the way that Joshua did since she had arrived at the cabin.

At the sound of a soft whistle, Beth looked toward the kitchen to where Holly stood. She gave a silent "thumbs up" and then went back to her duties.

Joshua pulled out her chair so that Beth could sit. He seated himself across from her, managing to look comfortable yet handsome at the same time.

"So tell me more about your Father and this cabin. Holly told me about the Mercy Gate this morning." Beth glanced over at the large wooden door, opened to reveal a gold gate that sparkled with the reflection of the colored lights from outside. The gate boasted an intricate lion's head in the center with eyes that were brilliant as diamonds.

"My Father resides here when he needs to rest. He also gave it to me to share with my Bride. As I mentioned, he was invited to other homes. However, the people soon forgot his nature, and he doesn't go there as often when they become dogmatic as to how the houses should be furnished. One house had a grand piano donated by someone, but no one could agree where it should go. Finally, in desperation, my Father put it in the pool." They both laughed as they imagined this.

Hesitating a moment, Beth pondered her next question. "And where is your Bride? Why isn't she here?"

Joshua paused. "I guess you could say that she's a work in progress. She needs to change some things before she can be my Bride. Actually, she's very much like the homes I described."

"That's a little brash, don't you think?" Beth asked.

"If she is to oversee this cabin with me, she needs to know how to do so effectively. We can't have any compromise as it will ruin the cabin's integrity. As you can see, everything is spotless."

Beth had already noticed the high standards of cleanliness at the cabin. Even the people, if that's in fact what they were, had "something" unusual about them that felt special.

"What is she like now?"

"She's a prostitute."

Shocked, Beth's eyes widened. "And she's your Bride?"

"Yes, she is. She can't fully commit to me, no matter what she does. She is sweet, but her heart still won't let go of her past or of her pain. Her heart is like those that build homes for my Father to dwell in. She desires anything but what I can give her."

"And you love her anyway?"

"Yes, I do."

Dinner arrived, served by Holly, and was as scrumptious as Beth had thought it would be. By the time Holly brought out dessert and tea, she simply picked at the pastry, too full to eat much more. They continued the enjoyable conversation until Beth excused herself for bed. Thanking Joshua, she made her way upstairs to her room where Celeste was drawing her bath. She sank into the tub, relaxing in the luxurious scents.

Once she exited the warmth of the tub, she pulled on her robe. Within moments, she dressed for bed and exhausted, fell into the silky sheets. She quickly succumbed to sleep, dreaming of the last days with her parents.

She saw herself sitting by her dad's bed during his final hours. She held his hand as he peacefully took his last breath. Looking at the closet in his room, she saw a being there right at that moment. The entity seemed full of light. A shadow stepped forward, that same familiar presence, somehow comforting her. As a hand reached out to her father, she watched as he rose up to take the hand in his own.

She woke briefly, then slept again. In the second dream, Beth again sat with her mother during her final hours, singing their favorite childhood songs. Beth glimpsed a figure by the closet out of the corner of her eye. When she looked again, the identity of the familiar shape was undeniable. It was Joshua, wearing a white robe and holding his hand out to her mother. Anger welled up in her along with the tears as her mother rose to meet him. Choking back the sobs, she didn't understand why he was taking her mother away from her. Hadn't she been faithful to him? Why did he have to take the only person she had left to protect her from the harsh realities of life? He had stolen her world for himself.

Waking with a start, she began grabbing what little she had brought with her, dressing in a pair of jeans, a plain t-shirt and a sweater, leaving everything that Joshua had provided for her. Fear gripped her as she dashed out of the cabin. The still and moonless night wrapped her in its arms, trying to calm her. Ignoring the nagging feeling to think this through rationally, she slowed as she reached Doubters' Hollow.

As she approached the edge of the forest, she could hear their voices.

At first, she tiptoed, hoping that she wouldn't draw attention to herself. Although it was behind her, she kept the cabin in sight, using the twinkling colored lights to guide her. But once she stepped into the forest, it grew too dark. By now, she was used to the rocks along the narrow trail and the sound of her footsteps on the soft dirt. She heard the whispers of the Doubters above her as they moved from limb to limb through the trees. A deafening sound crashed through the forest in her direction, silencing the voices.

"So you're running away, I see." A voice in the dark boomed. "Couldn't take all the goody two shoes and their so-called perfect ways, could you?"

Beth ignored the mocking words, concentrating on where she was walking. Tentatively feeling for the stones that lined the path, she didn't dare turn to the left or the right for fear she would lose her way. She had never realized how narrow the path was until she missed an area with no rock to guide her along the path for several steps.

"Looks like the princess is unguarded this evening." The voice behind her mocked her efforts. "What did he do? Promise something from that Book of his and then change his mind?"

Beth was silent. She shivered at the breath of someone--or something--on her neck, despite its warmth.

"Once they leave, they never come back." Another voice joined in, scoffing along with the first Doubter. The words tried to penetrate Beth's heart, but she knew they weren't true. After all, she had made it through here before. Beth found another opening and could hear more rustling in the trees. Fear again enveloped her as she uncertainly picked her way between the rocks. Were the side paths growing wider? If she wasn't careful, a wrong turn meant that she would wander a long time in this place. More voices joined in the taunting as the sound behind her approached. A familiar fragrance from her childhood wafted toward her from the distance. She recalled the lavender outside the forest entrance when she first arrived. Unbidden, Merle's words came to mind. He was right. She needed to use her senses to escape the forest.

When she reached the other side of the forest, she saw the lights of the city twinkling in the distance. She blinked for just a second. For a fleeting moment, she thought of the invitation from her co-worker to join them at "Shenanigan's." Suddenly, foul smells permeated her senses. Opening her eyes once more, she found herself downtown at midnight. The smells of the city reeked of cigarettes and booze, and for a moment, she wanted to go back to the cabin where she felt safe.

Instead, setting her hesitations aside, she walked into the bar, found her co-workers and sat down. Sara gave her a questioning look, and Beth mouthed back to her, "later." They talked and listened as the band played.

While Awaken Insurance provided medical coverage for its clients, the company also helped those who wanted to stop habits that were keeping them from living a healthy lifestyle. Although frowned upon somewhat, going to a night club on a Friday night was not discouraged. However, employees weren't supposed to discuss these weekend activities in the inner sanctum.

For the next two hours, Beth focused on forgetting the past week. Joshua had broken her trust in him--and broken her heart in the process.

However, just after 2:00 a.m., she looked toward the

door as he strode towards her. He didn't condemn any of the patrons, but some of them felt guilty and quickly exited the building. Joshua sat down at the table with the other girls without a word. Conversation screeched to an abrupt halt as the women were afraid of what the boss's son would say to them.

Still, Joshua kept his mouth closed, looking at each one, especially Beth, the compassion overflowing from his eyes.

Her own sense of betrayal tugging at her consciousness, Beth gazed into the same eyes that she had seen in her dream. His eyes held a love she had never known before, and without warning, fear suddenly overwhelmed her.

"Do you want to talk?" Joshua asked. "I know you have questions."

Beth excused herself, ignoring the giggles of her friends, as Joshua led her to a quiet table. Dressed in a short-sleeved polo shirt and blue jeans, he seemed unaware or at least unconcerned about his surroundings. He looked compassionately at anyone who walked by, despite their curious expressions at the two of them.

"Who are you to take my mother and my father when I needed them most?"

"It wasn't my choice. You know how sick they were. Because of their faithfulness to the Father, I ushered them into his presence. Their time was nowhere near done here on earth. But their illness was too great. You know how much they loved you and how concerned

Cheryl Olson

they were about how you handled their deaths. They
wanted me to stay with you, but I couldn't. Instead, I
sent someone else who could." Joshua paused for a
moment, gauging Beth's reaction. "Beth, you became a
doubter when you allowed fear to drive you from the
cabin."

"When you arrived, you had a different type of fear--
awe and reverence toward me. When you left, your fear
changed. We don't experience that type of fear in the
cabin because it's based on doubt. Zach came to the
cabin out of reverence, not doubt, as he chose to learn
of me. You need to have the same attitude–one of awe
and not doubt--if you are to reside in the cabin."

"You're kicking me out?" Beth looked at him with an
incredulous expression.

"No, Beth, of course not. You are always welcome,
no matter what you feel in your heart, but I know that if
you are fearful and if you believe that I'm an
intimidating person, you won't be comfortable there."
Joshua paused. "Look around at your friends and the
others. They feel shame and guilt for being here, yet I
haven't said a word." His gaze took in the scene and the
bar's patrons. "That fear rejects the love I truly have for
each and every person."

"Can I get you two something to drink?" A waitress
sauntered up to the table.

Joshua smiled up at her. "I'll have your best wine."

"I'm sorry, sir, we are out of that tonight. Can I
interest you in something else?"

"I'll just take a glass of water, then."

The waitress left and returned with a pitcher of water and a couple of glasses. As she poured the water from the pitcher to the glass, the liquid changed to a deep, rich bourbon wine color. The server stepped back in astonishment, spilling the water onto the table. "What the...." she exclaimed.

Shocked, Beth just sat there, mouth agape. Joshua chuckled and offered the waitress a drink.

"I can't. It's against the bar's policy."

"I'll try it." A gentleman came up to the table, and she introduced him as the owner. After one sip, he proclaimed, "This is the best wine we've ever served!" He turned to announce his discovery to those around him. But when he glanced back at the table, Joshua was once again gone.

As Beth sipped her wine, she realized how sweet it was. The blend of flavors hinted of several fruits, and she couldn't quite put her finger on the distinctive taste. She had never tasted anything like it before.

She heard a familiar voice and noticed that Holly was cleaning the counter at the bar. Beth sat back, watching quietly as Holly interacted with the customers.

"Can I get you something, sir?" Holly asked as she put away some glasses on a rack above her.

Dressed in a red plaid shirt and dark blue jeans, the man at the counter slumped over the bar as he struggled to catch his breath. With his unkempt blond hair, he looked as if he hadn't slept in days.

"I'll take a strawberry martini," he replied.

"Tough day?"

"You could say that. Too many thoughts swirling around in my head. I'm a lumberjack. A few months ago, I was cutting a tree and fell, and the electric saw brushed my right leg, taking off several layers of skin. It's infected, and I just found out I might have to have it amputated." He clarified, tears starting to form. "My wife took on a second job to help pay the bills since I'm not working, and I rarely see her."

"Oh, honey, I'm so sorry. Your drink is on the house. I also want to give you something a little extra to help you cope." Holly laughed as she looked at his shocked expression. "Oh, I know how that must sound. I make this completely natural product, a wild rose essence, so that people have more freedom in their thoughts, especially when they are under stress and have tough decisions to make." Holly explained as she finished mixing his drink. She pulled out a bottle and handed it to him. "I can't serve this to you, but you can put it in your drink. Use four drops at a time." He added the drops as she suggested. As he continued ordering drinks, he added more drops each time.

"Thanks, Holly! The drinks were wonderful! I know I'm going through a tough time, but you've given me hope, darlin,'" he smiled as he rose from his stool.

"I'll be with you during this time. You will know when I'm near." Holly grabbed her bag from under the counter, walking out from behind the bar.

"I'll be back soon, Joe. Thanks for tonight."

"Thank you, Holly!" The owner's voice boomed from the back. "I don't know how you do it. You come to one of the darkest places in the city and just shine and bless my customers."

"I specialize in bringing light to dark places, Joe. I've done it for years. That's who I am."

Holly walked over to Beth. "Are you ready to go?"

"I'm not going back to the cabin. I'll be going to a beach house where I'll be staying until my home is rebuilt. But thank you for taking care of me." Beth rose to give Holly a hug.

"Honey, I'm coming with you. It's late, and I'm sticking with you like glue. Joshua insisted that I keep you company."

"He won't force me to go back?"

"Never. He's about everyone making their own choices. However, you always have to face the consequences as a result of the choices you make."

Beth thought about the Doubters' Hollow. Nothing in the world could be that bad, or so she thought.

It took till after 4:00 a.m. for Beth to finally settle in at the beach house. Holly took the bedroom next to hers, and Beth could hear Holly's whispers. The ocean waves crashed wildly as Beth lay in bed, listening. She couldn't stop thinking about the dream. Why did Joshua rob her of her parents and leave her alone to fend for herself? His explanation was plausible, but then, he could have healed them, too. After all, she just watched

Cheryl Olson

him turn water into wine at a bar. None of it made any sense. She was barely out of her teens when she lost them. Because of their deaths--because of Joshua--she had become an adult, overnight, it seemed.

She thought about what Holly had told her about Joshua letting people make their own choices. He even let his Bride-to-be walk away from him.

The glass breaking downstairs startled Beth, and she jumped out of bed and rushed to see what happened. Upon viewing the wet floor, she realized that it was pouring down rain and that the fierce wind had broken the window. She called out to Holly for help, but as Beth looked outside, she thought she saw Holly walking on the shore. The high waves and the ferocity of the storm collided with the surf, making visibility next to impossible. As Beth watched, she feared that the current would carry Holly out to sea. But Holly stood firm. When another figure appeared, Beth knew immediately who it was. Trembling in the cold, Beth realized that the broken window was letting in the rain. Still, she watched Holly and Joshua standing on the shore, mesmerized as it seemed that the storm blew right through them.

Shaking herself from her reverie, Beth stood up to clean the mess. But something hit her from behind, and she saw white stars blinking before she completely blacked out.

PART 2 - BETH'S WORLD

CHAPTER 4

Beth inhaled and coughed again, gagging at the strong and not altogether unpleasant smell of antiseptic. Groggy and a bit confused after the incident, she recognized the familiar beep of a monitor. She slowly opened her eyes, taking in her surroundings. Sara sat quietly reading a magazine.

"Sara? What am I doing here?"

"They mostly brought you in for observation. A

board hit you from behind at the beach house, knocking you out. Maggie found you when the alarm went off last night, alerting the office that someone else was there." Sara replied.

"I was with Holly. She and Joshua had walked down to the beach. Joshua and I are upset with each other. I thought it would be best if I stayed at the beach house."

"I was at the nightclub when Joshua turned the water into wine. How did he do that?" Sara asked. "I was going to ask, but when I looked up, he had disappeared."

"Yeah, my new friends tend to do that." Beth sighed.

"Sara, I need to be alone for a while. Could you find my doctor or a nurse?"

"Sure. Are you okay?"

"Yes, just trying to process everything that's happened. I have no place to go when I leave here. I'm sure the beach house is unusable now because of the broken windows. And I left the cabin."

"You can come and stay with me." Sara invited as she rose to leave.

"Are you sure? I don't want to intrude." Beth worried.

"Of course! I would love to have you for as long as you need to stay."

"Thank you." Beth sighed in gratitude, the effort draining her further.

"Joshua," Beth whispered when Sara left to go find a nurse. She sat up, checking out the room but saw nothing. "Merle? Gabe? Holly?" She was in tears as she called out their names. She felt the presence of something and a scent that taunted her with its familiarity. It was Holly. Beth couldn't see her, but she knew Holly was there. She lay back down, smelling the scents in the room. "I feel so alone. I hope you understand why I can't come back. I don't know why, but something doesn't mesh with what I've been telling myself for years. If you or Joshua didn't cause my parents' sickness, who did?"

Beth paused for a minute to regain control of her emotions. Then, she addressed Joshua. "They were faithful to you and your Father to the end. You took them away from me, and I can't forgive you for that. I don't even know how to start." Beth lay in silence, waiting for a response. She knew that Joshua would never leave her or forsake her, but until this question was resolved between them, she sensed the rift of separation building.

She had experienced heaven, and it was at her fingertips. She still hesitated to take advantage of everything Joshua offered. She didn't realize all the options that awaited her.

Beth was released from the hospital a few hours later. Sara offered again to take her to her own home.

"I don't want to put you out. And what if Raul finds out? You know how the company feels about employees getting too close to each other." Beth worried when they were in Sara's car. "I could just stay at a motel."

"Nonsense! I have plenty of room. Besides, my home has been too quiet lately." Sara insisted as she pulled into her driveway.

As quiet and reserved as Sara was, she enjoyed making others feel at home. Beth wished Sara would open up more, but she preferred to keep to herself. Even so, her kind actions spoke volumes. Still, Beth longed to be needed by others.

Beth was still uncertain about all that had happened. She felt a little bit of déjà vu as she went through the evening activities with Sara, making dinner, mostly a homemade soup that Sara had previously canned herself. Her backyard garden was flourishing and beautiful. Sara enjoyed the natural aspects of creation, and she was a homebody for the most part. Her home was small, similar to Beth's, and very comfortable.

Beth gazed around the kitchen, looking at the updated appliances: the controlled temperature refrigerator and conventional oven. She could tell that Sara loved to cook and spent lots of time in this room. The kitchen also boasted a special canning cupboard where she kept her canning jars, a pressure canner and water bath canner. Sara spent time on the hobby of food preservation, and Beth sensed her love for the craft.

Beth tossed and turned all night, resulting in an aching back the following morning. Her head was still sore from the whack it took with the board. Sara did her best to comfort her friend. Although Beth was grateful, Sara's efforts didn't cover the loss she felt on top of the physical pain she was suffering. Underneath it all, she worried that the intruder might return. She didn't know how she would protect herself if he--or she--did.

The pair spent Sunday sitting around the house, watching movies and eating homemade pizza.

"Do you find it rather unusual that the company frowns on several things that we seem to do anyway?" Beth asked Sara.

"What do you mean?" Sara asked.

"Well, for one here we are, sitting and watching a movie. When I was a child attending church, we weren't allowed to go to the movie theater because what you were watching could stay with you forever if the Savior returned and took you to heaven. You might wake up every morning with the last scene you watched. That's what they told us, anyhow."

Sara laughed. "If that were the case, when I said 'shit' in the kitchen as I pulled pizza out of the oven, and the rapture happened, I'd see the curse word everywhere I went when I walked the streets of gold." The two of them laughed.

Sara seemed a bit edgy, and the fact that she burned her hand didn't help matters any. Over the last couple of weeks, Beth had noticed that Sara seemed really distracted. In fact, now that she thought about it, her lack of focus started when Merle and Gabe had arrived. She blamed it on their lack of compliance with the company dress code, but something about the entire situation still troubled her.

Beth questioned her about it.

"Just a minute. I have something to show you." Sara

Cheryl Olson

left the room and came back with a folder.

"Are those the photos from the company retreat we took about six months ago?" Beth asked as Sara opened the folder, and some photos slipped on the floor.

Sara nodded as she bent down to pick them up. "There was a notice that I needed to send some photos upstairs so that upper management could make up a bulletin board for the lobby area. I gave them most of what I had but kept out a few that were troubling me."

Beth looked over the photos. "I'm not sure what I'm looking at." She noticed several of the people sitting at various tables on the last night of the retreat.

"Look closer." Sara pointed to a table where the floor managers sat. Beth and Sara sat at a nearby table. Beth remembered Sara continuing to take pictures even though she seemed to have plenty.

Beth looked closer at the spot in one of the photos where Raul and Maggie sat. She could just make out their clasped hands under the table. Beth gasped.

"Seriously?"

"I don't know what to do. Headquarters wanted to see who all was at the dinner, and I had snapped several photos. I wasn't even paying attention while doing it."

"And they would notice this for sure." Beth replied. "Do either Raul or Maggie know that you have these?"

"I'm not sure. I haven't said anything to anyone until now. I thought about giving this to Merle or Gabe when they were there. I wanted to ask them how to handle it, but by the time I made the decision, they had left."

"If I were still in contact with Joshua, I'd give it to him." Beth looked at the photo again, the regret written on her face.

On Monday, the day dragged for Beth, and her throbbing head made matters worse. She longed to go back to Sara's and rest. When the day ended, relief washed over Beth.

"I think I will walk by my property and pick up my car before heading back to your place." Beth told Sara as she grabbed her jacket from the coat room in the lobby.

"That's quite a distance from the office," Sara observed. "Mind if I walk with you?"

"I'd love that." Beth exclaimed as they left the building. "It's a wonderful walk and a beautiful day. You miss so much when you're in the car."

They walked by the church where Beth had been just a few days before with Joshua. "Joshua helped build this church." Beth told Sara as they stopped. After chatting for a few minutes more, the two decided to go inside. Sara was surprised that Beth went in as if she owned the place but followed her anyway. "Doesn't Maggie's husband pastor this church?"

"Yes, he does. He's a good friend of Joshua's." Beth answered.

Beth walked up to the front, staring again at the picture that was on the wall behind the pulpit. "The congregation didn't seem to want him here, and they kicked him out. When Maggie's husband came, he invited Joshua back, but Joshua refused unless the rest of the congregation believed in him as well. Still, Joshua visits the pastor all the time."

"How sad that Joshua isn't welcomed here even though he built this church. I thought Christians were supposed to love everyone. Instead, I guess they mostly just tolerate others."

Beth turned around to gaze at Sara sitting in one of the pews. "It seems that way, Sara." Beth observed sadly. "I thought Joshua was about love as well, but he seems to like to give us pain even though he claims to love us."

"That doesn't sound like a friend who I would want to have supporting me, Beth," Sara answered. "Maybe the church had their reasons. It's been a long time since I've been in a church."

"Why did you leave?" Beth questioned.

"I wasn't welcome because of my lifestyle. I used to do drugs and party. Besides, I have two piercings, even though you can't see them. Not to mention the butterfly tattoo on my shoulder. And another tattoo I'd rather forget about."

"And that kept you from coming to church?"

Sara nodded, her sadness written on her face. "In fact, it almost kept me from working at the office. No one knows about the piercings or the tattoos. It's on my shoulder, so it's usually covered. I got it in memory of someone I was once close to."

"I'm sorry that you felt rejection from the church because of something so minor. From what I've learned of Joshua and the others, that should never happen, not even at work."

"So why doesn't Joshua pick you up anymore? I figured he was kind of sweet on you."

"I was kind of hoping. But then, I found out something that changed everything." Beth sighed. "I don't think I can ever trust him again."

"Well, at least you can tell it's not a cultish commune at the cabin." Sara commented as they started to leave.

"Why is that?"

"They haven't tried to take you back."

As Beth and Sara were leaving the church, Beth walked ahead of Sara. A shot fired behind her. When she turned, Sara's body lay lifeless on the ground, the blood pooling at her feet.

Beth sunk to the ground in horror, shocked at the suddenness of her friend's death. Sirens blared across the distance, but she had no idea who called emergency personnel. She simply waited in grief by her friend's still body, alternating between sobs and complete disbelief.

Hours later, the police were gone, but they had sealed off the church building. Maggie and pastor stayed with Beth until the police finished talking to her. They offered her a place to stay.

When the hours of interrogation finally ended, Beth faced a greater quandary than ever. Tears continued to streak down her cheeks. Where were those that promised to care for her? Why was she alone again?

She felt the same fear and anger at what must have

been a dream when she saw Joshua at her mother's death bed. She saw what Joshua was capable of and felt even more alone than before. Did anything or anyone stand for what they said? Joshua had three of her loved ones now. If he loved her so much, why did he want her alone like this?

However, the detective strongly advised her against going with Maggie and pastor. The police still didn't know the motive behind Sara's murder. If it were an intentional act toward the church and the pastor's family, he recommended that they all stay at a safe house. Beth just shook her head as the tears continued to flow.

"What are your plans right now, Beth?" The officer's concerned tone just made Beth cry all the more.

"I was on my way to my house to get my car when this happened," she managed to say between sobs.

"Come on. I'll be happy to give you a ride."

Once they arrived, she stood next to her car that was still parked at the side of the road. Tears streamed down her face. The police officer just waited, not able to provide much emotional support.

She crawled into her car in her confusion, waiting for an answer that she didn't think would ever come. First, she drove to a nearby rest area. After stopping the car and looking around, she noticed a couple of men with blankets talking just a few feet from her car door. Sighing, she started up her vehicle and drove to the park where she and Joshua had talked. Taking her keys out of the ignition, she made sure her doors were tightly closed and locked. Huddling under her coat, she finally fell into a fitful sleep.

***

Looking over the roofs of the nearby houses, Holly and Joshua gazed down at the sleep figure. Tears filled Holly's eyes. "Please, Joshua!" she begged. "Let me bring her back to the cabin!"

Joshua shook his head in discouragement. "You know she has to return on her own. I'll let you know when it's time to do more. Right now, she has to walk out the choices she made in her doubt." Though Joshua's voice was stern, it was filled with compassion. Watching her in such grief pained him as much as it did Holly, probably even more.

Holly looked over at her companion and at the wet streaks streaming down his cheeks.

CHAPTER 5

"Well, I guess there's a first time for everything," Beth thought to herself, taking in the dusty interior of her car. She had never slept in her vehicle before. Despite the craziness of all that had happened over the past few days, she felt the peace of watching another sunrise. Even so, her head was pounding, and she'd had no time to pack aspirin or any extra clothes. She didn't even have a fresh work suit with her. She started up the car

and drove up the road a little ways. Finding a diner, she went in to order breakfast.

She had to be at work in an hour but once again, considered her wrinkled suit. It certainly wouldn't do for the office.

Scrolling through her cell phone, she found her tailor's number and scheduled the delivery of two suits to the office upon her arrival. When she hung up, her thoughts once again returned to the cabin. Celeste had chosen the most exquisite gowns for her to wear at dinner. She looked again at her work jacket, now stained with Sara's blood, and touched her blond hair, hastily pulled back into a pony tail. As she took in her surroundings at the diner that she frequented, she noticed that her usual waitress hadn't provided the normal courteous service and seemed rushed and short-tempered.

"I know I look like a mess. To say it's been a rough week is certainly an understatement." Beth chuckled to herself. Her week had been more like a nightmare.

Without a word, the waitress put her check on the table and walked away. Beth turned it over and took out some money. She pulled out enough cash for her meal and a small tip, leaving nothing in her wallet. Beth got up, grabbed her purse and left. As she hopped into her car, she noticed that the gas gauge was low as well. She hoped that she could make it to work. Beth beginning to feel as if she were a bad omen.

As she drove into the parking lot at work and got out

of her car, she caught her sleeve on the door, ripping it. That felt like the last straw. "Ugh! Why is this happening?" She got back inside, and pounded the steering wheel in frustration. Finally, she put her head down on the steering wheel and sobbed once again.

Just as she felt the loneliness overwhelm her, she felt a hand on her shoulder. Although she knew no one was there, she still turned around to check out the back seat. Still, the perfume of honeysuckle and jasmine, her mother's favorite scents, filled the car.

Through the tears, she smiled. She knew that Holly was near, making her presence known. Composing herself, she gathered her belongings to prepare for the day.

Despite the comforting fragrance and reassurance of Holly's nearness, Beth still felt alone as she walked through the front door of the office complex. Still dressed in her wrinkled and blood-stained work suit and trying to hide the rip on her sleeve, she stumbled through the building, looking for the suits she had ordered. Other employees glanced sideways at her or avoided her completely. The feeling of camaraderie that she formerly felt with her co-workers seemed to fade.

Maggie took one look at her and frowned. "A delivery came for you about a half hour ago. I hope it's the proper clothing for the inner sanctum as I can't let you in like that." She paused, looking at the floor. "Again, I'm so sorry about Sara. I know how close you two were."

Beth went to the manager's desk, and Maggie handed her the garment bag. "Thanks, Maggie. Any messages?"

"Just one. And to be honest, after last night, it really scared me, too." Maggie turned to the mail cubicle behind her.

Beth read the note in her hand. "You're next if you tell, bitch." She dropped the piece of paper as if it had burned her. Beth gasped, smiling weakly and picking up the note. Fear grabbed her, and she backed up against a wall to steady herself.

"Are you okay, Beth?" Maggie queried. "Do you need some water?"

"I - I'm fine. Yes, please. Water will be fine. If you don't mind, I need to change. If anyone or anything comes for me, please have security check it out first. I wish I didn't have to be at work today, no matter what the rules are around here. Even so, I have no idea of where I'd stay."

Maggie got Beth a bottle of water. Beth went to the restroom on the first floor where she changed. She quickly washed up and found a rubber band and some hairpins in her purse to arrange her hair in a bun. She added some blush to brighten her cheeks and dabbed a little mascara on her lashes to hide the tired look in her eyes. She powdered her red nose and around her eyes from the tears she had shed through the night and this morning.

She thought about her encounter with Maggie. She

had never had a problem with passing into the inner sanctum before. Maggie's comment rubbed her the wrong way, and she wondered if she was being overly sensitive. She began to compare her feelings with what Merle and Gabe had gone through weeks ago--rejection as none of them fit in.

She now knew now that the company house on the beach was some sort of time warp, even with Holly there. On the other hand, the cabin and Doubters' Hollow was real. She shivered when she thought about the Hollow. She knew she still doubted Joshua's true identity, and she didn't feel that he was what he appeared to be. Were the Doubters right? Who was really free?

She heard the office clock strike 8:00 a.m. and exited the restroom. Maggie had left another bottle of water sitting at her desk along with a bottle of aspirin.

When Beth took the elevator to the third floor and walked to her cubicle, a bouquet of flowers greeted her. The attached card simply read, "Our sincere sympathy for the loss of a wonderful woman in our company. Please give our regards to her family."

Still in a daze, Beth pulled out her chair to sit down at her desk. Sara had no family. She had moved to the area and never said where she came from nor talked about her past. The fact that they were both isolated from others somehow knit them together as best friends. Beth had no idea of who to contact as Sara never used an address book. She only used emails for business.

Cheryl Olson

While her cell phone might have had contact information inside, the police had confiscated that, looking for clues.

Other members of the inner sanctum wandered in and out of the area by Sara's cubicle, dropping off stuffed animals, flowers and cards. Several made small talk with Beth. The police had already taken Sara's computer as evidence, but Beth didn't think they'd find much on it except work files.

The floor manager, Raul, stopped by after a while and checked on Beth as she entered client information into the data base.

Beth admired the company since her parents had worked there for many years. Naturally, Beth followed in her parents' footsteps and enjoyed a successful career with the company as well. With the exception of the events surrounding the fire and even in the handling of Sara's death, the company had come alongside Beth and other employees as they faced various life events--births, weddings and funerals.

Beth took a quick break, returning to her cubicle after just few minutes. She noticed Raul rummaging through her desk as he appeared to look for something. When he saw Beth, he started, quickly slamming the drawer shut. With a guilty expression, he stopped what he was doing. "I was so sad to hear about Sara. She was a wonderful worker. The police are asking for her computer and her notes to see if they can figure out who did this to her.

"The company wishes they could do more, but because of the suspicious circumstances of her death, our hands are tied. I mean, we can't let it out that an employee was *murdered*!" The office manager whispered the last word. "I can hardly believe that you were there when it happened. That breaks my heart, but you do understand that Sara was involved in some questionable situations that did not comply with our company policies for employees."

"What are you saying?" Beth looked shocked.

"We had our concerns about Sara and about what she was involved in. The rumors include sinister activities and possibly even drugs. What did you know about that? Are you involved, too?" He stared at Beth accusingly.

Confused, Beth stammered, "Um, uh, Sara just off...offered her home so that I could relax after the fire. Unfortunately, I didn't relax much."

"Beth, I know that you are going through a trying time yourself. But you shouldn't burden your co-workers with your problems." Raul advised as he pulled the chair from Sara's cubicle over to Beth's and sat down. "You haven't had any threatening emails from clients, have you?"

"No. I haven't." Beth shook her head to emphasize the point.

"Have you read the company manual recently?"

"I read it regularly. Why?"

"I'm concerned about your friendship with Sara.

Granted she worked here for five years and was a wonderful employee, but if she's involved in something sinister in her own time, I wonder about your involvement as well." Raul explained. "After all, we have a reputation to uphold."

"Why does that affect the company? It refers to our clients--those we manage the funds for, not those we work with. The only exceptions are for fraternizing. Sara wasn't involved in anything questionable as far as I know."

"Even so, I'm relieving you of your duties for the day. Go to the company conference room and reread the manual instead. Write up a report for me and give it to me by the end of the day. We must follow the manual to the letter. The owners had their top men here last week, checking us out as you well know. I understand they invited you to stay with them at Joshua's home. We missed several points, but granted, the manual is so old, it's amazing we could still decipher it." Raul observed. Getting up from the chair, he returned to Sara's cubicle. "Are you still staying at Joshua's?"

"No. I'll stay at a motel until my house is built. The insurance is covering that. Bad things happen when I'm with my friends, and I don't want to put anyone else at risk." Beth responded sadly.

"Do the police know if the fire at your house is connected to Sara's murder?" Raul questioned.

Beth thought for a moment. "I hadn't even thought about it. Do you think it's a possibility? Will they look into it?"

"I will personally check on it for you." The floor manager replied.

"I'll keep that in mind." Beth answered.

Beth went to the conference room and found the plain white manual, just as Raul said. She grabbed a water and a pack of almonds to snack on while she studied. The rest of the day passed uneventfully. When Beth called the front desk, she had no new messages, which was a relief after this morning. She then called a local motel not far from the office and reserved a room for a few nights.

Beth closed down her computer for the night after spending the day reviewing the manual. She dropped off a note on Raul's desk, stating that she would finish the report by the next day and placed the manual in a bag to take home with her. Leaving out the front door with her co-workers to the garage, she stayed silent, worn out by all that had transpired.

Upon seeing her car, she let out a small cry. Someone had taken a screwdriver and scratched the paint in the driver's side and slashed two of the tires. Beth did the only thing she knew to do next. As she held back the tears for what seemed like at least the tenth time that day, she called the detective handling Sara's murder. As she related the events of the day, she remembered the cryptic phone message that she had received that morning. When she told him about it, he questioned her further, but she could provide little information. He tried to calm her fears with little success.

Beth opened the glove compartment to pull out her insurance card to show the detective when he arrived. As she reached into her purse, she felt an unfamiliar yet bulky shape. Digging a little further, she pulled out a handwritten envelope addressed to her in Sara's handwriting. She looked at it with interest, turning it over before stuffing it into her skirt pocket.

CHAPTER 6

Once the detective arrived, she showed him the damage to her vehicle. Upon hearing that she had reservations at the hotel, he quickly cancelled her plans. "I'm genuinely afraid for your safety, Beth. Let me take you to a safe house where we can protect you."

Beth was in no mood to argue and welcomed the officer's kind concern. She sank into the back seat of the squad car, closing her eyes as the officer drove.

The cozy front porch boasted a small coffee table, and two chairs completed the ensemble. Inside, the worn furnishings promised her a comfortable stay. Although the refrigerator didn't provide much in the way of food, the contents were practical and nourishing--a vegetable tray, eggs, cheese and cold cuts.

The detective gave Beth strict orders not to leave the premises without an officer present. Two officers provided a solid presence, one inside to visit with and the other outside, standing guard.

"*At least I have a bed to sleep in,*" Beth thought.

Beth walked into the tiny kitchen, turning around and touching all the appliances in every direction. After brewing a cup of tea, she took out the envelope from her pocket and sat down in a recliner in the living room.

> *Dear Beth,*
>
> *I am truly sorry to involve you in this, but you are the only person that I know who will do the right thing, the only person that I trust at this point.*
>
> *The evidence of Raul and Maggie's affair is right there in the photos in plain view. You have seen them for yourself. For months, I hid the pictures and never said anything, but Raul knew that I had them. He threatened me, hoping to recover the photos, but I told him that I would never give them up.*
>
> *I feel as if someone is watching me, so I hid*

them in the church the other day when you and I were there. For a while, I wondered why I should bother, and I felt like giving in. I thought about just handing the pictures over to him. But as I pondered the matter further, I changed my mind. In my heart of hearts, I knew I had to do the right thing. I couldn't let Raul--and his evil plans--win.

I need to finish this note. In the morning, I'll be gone. Don't look for me as you won't be able to find me. I have my own secrets that I hope you never know. I don't want to create further complications and think this is for the best.

Go get the pictures as soon as you can. They are at the church, taped under the third pew from the front on the left.

I will miss you so much. You were the one bright light during my time here. Thank you for your friendship more than words can say. Sara

Beth folded the letter and put it back into the envelope. The note raised more questions than it answered. What had Sara gotten herself into? And did the pictures really put Sara at risk? What should she do now to keep the pictures--and herself--safe? This whole situation seemed to become more complicated by the minute. She wished she could talk to someone and process her feelings. Sighing, she thought again of

Joshua and his strong yet calming presence.

Beth contemplated what to do next. She knew that she had to recover the photos, but then what? Who would she give them to? They were obviously the motive behind Sara's murder and maybe even the reason that her own house had been burned down. Raul was behind all of this because he wanted to keep his affair with Maggie quiet.

While she wished for Joshua, the hurt in her heart prevented her from calling out to him. "Holly, if I ever needed you, now is that time!" Beth announced. "I know that you can tell me exactly what happened to Sara and why."

Beth went to the bedroom and sat quietly in the chair, waiting. She wasn't sure exactly what she expected--maybe to hear, feel or even smell something.

"What should I do?"

Again, nothing.

"Believe me, if I knew what to do, I would do it. But I'm stuck here. What's next?"

The bedroom door slowly creaked opened. Holly stood there, a warm glow surrounding her. She beckoned Beth to follow. Happy yet apprehensive, Beth rose from the recliner. Walking into the living room, she glanced at the officer, but he just smiled and waved, not seeming to notice anything amiss. She followed Holly down the steps to the sidewalk. The officer watching the house saw Beth but just nodded at her, never moving from his post.

Beth walked with Holly to the church, and Holly opened the door. She mouthed a silent "goodbye" to Beth and disappeared.

Shaking her head, Beth turned back to go inside. The entire building was dark except for a single street light shining through one of the many stained glass windows. She walked down the aisle in between the pews and found the third pew from the front on her left. Feeling her way around under the pew, she found the loose corner of the envelope containing the photos, just as Sara said.

Sitting in that same pew, Beth glanced through the photos again. Even though she knew about the affair and had seen most of these, she still couldn't believe the evidence in front of her own eyes.

As Beth continued to thumb through the pictures, she saw more evidence of the compromising position that Raul and Maggie had placed themselves in. The company manual grabbed her attention in one of the photos, and she went to the next one before stopping and checking again. She was so lost in her thoughts that she almost missed it.

The photo in question showed two copies of the employee manual. Although they looked nearly identical, she could tell that one of them didn't have the official gate logo on it, designed by her father. Thinking back to earlier in the day when Raul forced her to study the company manual again, she closed her eyes, remembering. The manual was plain with no logo on the

Cheryl Olson

front. Digging through her handbag, Beth pulled out the notebook to confirm her suspicions. Just as she thought, the logo was missing.

Beth continued to flip through the pictures. One of the photos showed the whole team at the round table, Raul and Maggie next to each other. She took a deep breath, trying to process all of this information.

The sound of a door creaking open startled her, and she jumped up, dropping the photos. Turning, she saw Raul with Maggie and some of the others that were in the last photo.

"I knew that Sara had involved you in this! I should have taken you out last night, too, since burning down your house wasn't enough." Raul's eyes were blazing. "Give me those pictures. Now!" Raul held a gun in his right hand, and he held Maggie's hand in his left.

Under her breath, Beth whispered Joshua's name. She looked around but saw no one. However, she kept her eyes on Maggie, who screamed. At the same time, she fell back, letting go of Raul's hand.

"What happened?" Raul asked, glancing at Maggie, who was now sobbing uncontrollably on the church floor. "Never mind her. I need those pictures."

"They don't belong to you. They're Sara's. I'm turning them over to headquarters. They can decide what steps to take next."

"Beth, you are really dense. I'm taking over the company. Tonight. And I know you're palling around with the Boss's son and will tell him everything anyhow." Raul scoffed at Beth's expression.

"But how....?"

"Beth! Don't say another word. This is between Raul and me." Beth turned to the front of the church where Joshua stood, dressed in a white robe.

With authority, Joshua walked down the steps of the altar and toward Raul. Raul stood indignant, unconcerned about Joshua's true identity. His voice changed into an ugly snarl, shaking Beth to the very core of her being.

"You have no right to be in this building, Joshua! The people kicked you out long ago!" he threatened.

"You are correct, Raul, as you saw to that when you lied to the congregation. You took away their freedom when you forced me out. But you will not take away my Father's business from him. He doesn't need the pictures anyhow as he knows all about your antics." "You cannot get to him without going through me." Joshua announced. His strong voice filled Beth with courage.

"If you die a second death, can I keep you in the grave this time?" Raul's tone deepened with the implied threat.

"No! Absolutely not! I conquered death once and for all."

"You took Beth's parents!" Raul sneered.

"I didn't cause their death, you did, satan!"

Beth looked back and forth between the pair, stunned by the revelation that their words implied. The colors of the stained glass blurred for a moment. She felt as if they were in another dimension instead of standing in the middle of the church. A misty fog seemed to settle over them all, making it difficult to see. Out of the corner of her eye, Beth noticed Maggie stirring on the floor and slowly walked over to her, not wanting to interrupt the argument between Joshua and Raul. She bent down on the floor next to Maggie who began to sit up. She reached down to help her up.

Raul's voice grew louder. "But you took them from me. I had them in my grasp, and you snatched them away."

"They never belonged to you. And neither does my Father's business. You need to leave this place. **Now**!"

Beth watched as more angels, led by Holly, surrounded Joshua, appearing from out of nowhere with swords in their hands. Raul snarled again and stormed out the door just as the police officers--the same ones that had been watching Beth at the safe house--arrived. Raul's jaw dropped to the floor, and his eyes filled with shock. The next thing Beth knew, Joshua was sitting on the steps of the altar. Raul tried to escape but stopped abruptly when he saw the police reaching for their guns on their hips. "We received a call that the suspect was here." One of them explained.

"He killed Sara!" Beth cried out, pointing at Raul. "And I think that he set my house on fire. He stole some pictures that Sara took at a company retreat. Make sure that you grab those since they are evidence, too."

Snatching the pictures from Beth, Raul tried to rip

them into tiny shreds, but a nearby officer pulled them out of his hands in the nick of time. He looked around for support from his cohorts, but they seemed to have scattered, leaving him alone. The officers surrounded him although he still held his gun in his hands. Grabbing at any last straw, he tried to take Maggie hostage, but she was with Beth at the front of the church, out of harm's way. Weighing his options, he retreated, dropping the gun and raising his hands in surrender.

Within minutes, the officers had read Raul his Miranda rights and handcuffed him, leading him out the door.

Beth looked at the altar where Joshua still sat on the steps, waiting for her. He was once again dressed in the familiar jeans and polo shirt that he wore the first day Beth met him instead of the robe he had just had on.

"Maggie, is your husband on his way?" he asked. His soft eyes filled with compassion as he spoke, and Maggie almost fell back at the overwhelming love she felt pulsing from his presence.

"Yes, Joshua, he is." Maggie looked at the floor, ashamed. "Do you think he will ever forgive me?"

"Yes, as he sorts things out over the next several months, he will come to his senses. Give him space as this will be a trying season for both of you. Even so, this will bring the revival that he's been praying for, the revival that I am calling him to pursue."

"Joshua! Great to see you!" Pastor rushed in through the front door. "When the police called to say we had a break in, I had no idea what was happening." He paused, staring at his wife. "Maggie what are you doing here? I didn't know that you were involved."

"Pastor, you need to wait until later to talk to your wife about this mess. Right now, I need you both to listen. What happens in your congregation over the next several months and years will depend on how you two work together. It will start this Sunday, and it's an answer to prayer--the deepest cry of your heart that you have both had for years. Go home, pray together and get some rest. The coming days will be a busy season for both of you in every way." The couple's serious expression mirrored Joshua's intensity as he spoke. "I need you to both focus on your love for my Father and for each other and work together on the coming revival."

Joshua bid them goodbye and watched as Pastor and Maggie quietly left the building, with their arms wrapped around each other.

Beth stood still, closing her eyes, afraid to even risk a look at Joshua. She felt so ashamed for being a doubter, for denying him for who he was and is. Then, she felt his quiet presence in front of her. She slowly opened her eyes and saw him standing there, reaching out his arms. She stepped into his safe embrace but then fell at his bare feet, crying and wiping her tears with her hair. "I am so sorry! Please forgive me!" She wept.

"Beth, my darling! Of course, I forgive you! I have loved you from the beginning of time. That will never change." Joshua bent down and picked up Beth, cradling her in his arms as he carried her up the steps to the altar. As they sat together, he wrapped his arms around her, holding her as he whispered sweetly into her ear. The room seemed to disappear as they sat, exchanging words of love and passion.

PART 3 - THE WEDDING

CHAPTER 7

Beth napped fitfully, exhaustion finally overtaking her. The last few days had been a whirlwind--selecting fabric for her wedding dress, fittings, reviewing etiquette and procedures for taking over as the lady of the cabin and the duties of ruling with Joshua. She hadn't had a spare moment to herself. She thought she heard a knock on her door but ignored it, settling back under the comfortable covers. Rap! Rap! Rap! More knocks followed. Beth sat up, frightened that she had missed it. Her beloved had come for her, but she wasn't ready. Rising from her bed, she opened the door, hoping to catch him. Tears flowed down her cheeks as she called out, "Joshua! My beloved! I'm sorry!" She dashed down the stairs to the deserted lobby. The two prayer warriors in the alcove were gone; Holly wasn't in the kitchen, and Celeste was missing from the clothing section. Beth hurried to the east side of the cabin where she noticed the opened wooden door, the gate ajar.

A scream woke her, and she realized she was hearing the sound of her own voice. "Beth, wake up!" Holly's voice pulled her back to consciousness. Beth opened her eyes. Looking around, she realized she was safely in her room at the cabin. She sat up and leaned into her friend's chest, crying. "I'm so glad it was a dream! Joshua came and knocked on the door, but I couldn't wake up in time. I ran downstairs, and even the prayer warriors were gone from the alcove, and the bowls of prayers had spilled over on the floor. The wooden door was open with the gate a jar. I felt so defeated."

"Oh, honey. You don't need to worry. Nothing can separate you from Joshua's love. You will be ready for him. We will make sure of it. Now, go dry your tears and come downstairs for a cup of tea."

"Alright." Beth rose, going into the bathroom to wash away her tears. She pulled back her hair back into a ponytail and touched up her make up. Her eyes were dry but tired and bloodshot. The long week had taken its toll on her.

A couple of days later, Joshua needed to finalize some business matters at Awaken Insurance. After he finished, Joshua dropped Beth off at the cabin before going to the village that she had seen the day she sat at the gazebo.

Joshua had left to stay with his Father. He was preparing a better place for them away from the cabin. The cabin was hers to oversee. She would take in the lost, those struggling to find their way through Doubters' Hollow. Still, she looked forward to the new home Joshua was building for them together. When it was ready, he would meet her at the gate and open it for the first time.

Holly was waiting for Beth, and the two of them walked down the stairs together. Holly motioned for her to stay in the dining area while she prepared tea.

When Beth entered the dining area, her parents, Sara, Merle and Gabe all sat there, waiting. Others who lived at the cabin were present as well. The dining area had been decorated for a bridal shower, but Beth didn't even notice as she was so focused on her mom and dad. Crying, she ran into her parents' arms.

"Oh, Beth, darling! We are so sorry that we couldn't come sooner," her mother sobbed. "Joshua asked us to keep our distance as you processed through our home goings. We hated watching you go through all that endured. The day you were sitting up at the gazebo, we saw you from the town square, but I think your eyes were blinded so that you couldn't see us. We tried so hard to get a closer look at you."

"I understand now what happened and why I needed to go through it. None of it was Joshua's doing. What happened had nothing to do with him. How I responded--the sadness, hurt and anger--was my own free will," Beth cried even harder as she grabbed a hand of each parent, hardly believing that they were there. The warmth and squeezes as she held theirs felt solid and true.

"Yes. Free will. In this way, the Father truly knows if our hearts are in line with him. You passed, my Sugar Plum." Beth smiled at the sweet nickname her father had called her since she was just a baby.

"Daddy, I never knew how close you were to the Father. Joshua told me about your encounter with Raul and his brother."

"Another great example of free will." Dave observed. "I should have followed protocol, but I was too excited about getting the Father to his company. I didn't see the whole picture. The three months that we spent at his friend's home opened my eyes. And when I danced before him in celebration, I really could not contain myself. It wasn't the building, but his presence that mattered. All he wanted was to walk with me closely."

Beth looked at her father as the tears welled up.

"Dad, you have such a heart for the Father. As a child, I couldn't understand what that meant. Instead, I thought that you were rejecting me for not being everything you desired. I know now that I was wrong, and it was about your passion and love for him instead. How wonderful!"

Beth turned to Sara as the tears continued to flow. They blessed each other. "You are a princess in the making." Beth declared. "I know that you really suffered even though I don't know all the details. Even so, I will do what I can to help you rectify all of that pain."

"Thank you, Beth, that sounds amazing!" Sara exclaimed.

"Beth! I just heard the shofar! Joshua's on his way!" Holly rushed into the dining room. "Celeste has your gown ready."

With quick hugs all around, Beth excused herself from her party and joined Holly and Celeste as they began to ready her for the wedding celebration. While she and her assistants had plenty of time to make everything perfect, it only took a matter of minutes.

The dress was made of the purest satin and hand-sewn lace. The hem and train were edged with roses, and petals covered the train, which filled the entire room. Holly and Celeste, with the help of Merle and Gabe, smoothed it out as it now covered the dining hall. The four of them helped carry it behind Beth as she proceeded to the gate.

Standing in anticipation, Beth grew nervous. What if he had changed his mind and found her not worthy of the task? She carried the church on her shoulders and would continue to do so whether or not she was his Bride. Hadn't He proved that there was no other? He loved her as Solomon had loved his bride.

As if he reading her thoughts, she heard his voice beyond the door. Opening the door, Joshua quoted from the Song of Solomon:

>"...*Until dawn breathes its light and night slips away. You're beautiful from head to toe, my dear love, beautiful beyond compare, absolutely flawless. Come with me from Lebanon, my bride. Leave Lebanon behind, and come. Leave your high mountain hideaway. Abandon your wilderness seclusion, Where you keep company with lions and panthers guard your safety. You've captured my heart, dear friend. You looked at me, and I fell in love. One look my way and I was hopelessly in love! How beautiful your love, dear, dear friend--far more pleasing than a fine, rare wine, your fragrance more exotic than select spices. The kisses of your lips are honey, my love, every syllable you speak a delicacy to savor. Your clothes smell like the wild outdoors, the ozone scent of high mountains. Dear lover and friend, you're a secret garden, a private and pure fountain.*
>
>*Body and soul, you are paradise, a whole orchard of succulent fruits--Ripe apricots and peaches, oranges and pears; Nut trees and*

cinnamon, and all scented woods; Mint and lavender, and all herbs aromatic; A garden fountain, sparkling and splashing, fed by spring waters from the Lebanon mountains."
Song of Solomon 4:7-15

Joshua stood at the gate, taking a deep breath before he unlocked the latch, pulling it out toward him. He did the same with the wooden door. He took her delicate hand in his, lovingly caressing it. He turned around, and together, they walked down the path that led to the altar.

Beth was mesmerized at the display in front of her. She had never seen the Father though she had heard much about him. As Joshua continued holding her hand, she walked in matched step with him. She began weeping despite herself. He truly was the Lion and the Lamb--her own Bridegroom.

While walking down the aisle with family and friends seated on either side of her, she recited the next section from the Song of Solomon:

"My dear lover glows with health--red-blooded, radiant! He's one in a million. There's no one quite like him! My golden one, pure and untarnished, with raven black curls tumbling across his shoulders. His eyes are like doves, soft and bright, but deep-set, brimming with meaning, like wells of water. His face is rugged, his beard smells like sage, His voice,

Cheryl Olson

his words, warm and reassuring.
Fine muscles ripple beneath his skin, quiet and beautiful.
His torso is the work of a sculptor, hard and smooth as ivory. He stands tall, like a cedar, strong and deep-rooted, A rugged mountain of a man, aromatic with wood and stone. His words are kisses, his kisses words.
Everything about him delights me, thrills me through and through! That's my lover, that's my man, dear Jerusalem sisters."
Song of Solomon 5:10-16

The wedding was more incredible than Beth had ever imagined. Even when the dinner ended, she still felt the anticipation building. She knew that in a few short hours, she would be with Joshua in the village home that he had built for them to share.

They had already discussed the plans and how they would work together. Although Beth was the Bride of Christ, many earthly matters needed to be taken care of, such as reuniting and restoring Sara's family so that they could join her in heaven. The restoration of Pastor and Maggie's marriage and facilitating the upcoming revival was also at the top of their priority list. Beth knew that there was even more, like finding the secret of Doubters' Hollow. It was time to clean the Father's houses and bring them into order and into all of the fullness that he had for them.

www.ingramcontent.com/pod-product-compliance
Lightning Source LLC
Chambersburg PA
CBHW071313200626
46813CB00015B/2118